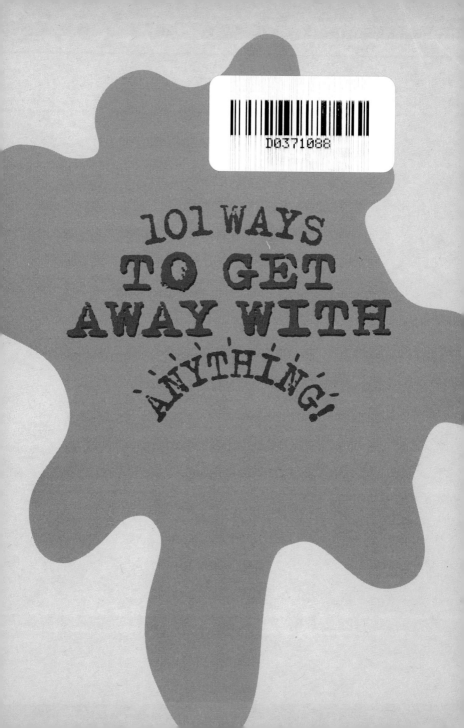

101 WAYS
TO GET
AWAY WITH
ANYTHING!

101 WAYS TO GET AWAY WITH ANYTHING!

By Malcolm with David Levithan

SCHOLASTIC INC.

New York   Toronto   London   Auckland
Sydney   Mexico City   New Delhi
Hong Kong   Buenos Aires

ISBN 0-439-35132-4

12 11 10 9 8 7 6 5 4 3 2 1   2 3 4 5 6 7/0

Printed in the U.S.A.

First Scholastic printing, February 2002

INTRODUCTION

Don't get me wrong. It's not like I get away with everything. But when you have a family like mine, you get to learn a few things. Or 101 . . . 202 . . . 303 . . . the number doesn't matter. What matters is whether you can pull off things you never thought you could pull off . . . without breaking a sweat.

Use these how-tos wisely. And whatever you do, don't let your teachers or parents go near them. The secrets need to stay safe with us.

— Malcolm

HOW TO DEAL WITH THE SCHOOL BULLY WHEN THE SCHOOL BULLY HAPPENS TO BE YOUR BROTHER

I happen to have firsthand experience with this one. Deep, deep down, I know my brother Reese is a nice guy. The problem is that he doesn't go deep, deep down very often . . . especially not when we're at school. So here's how you deal with this kind of situation.

1. Always be on the lookout for moments you can use against him. Is he singing in the shower? Tape it. Did he write a rough draft of a very bad love note? Steal it from the trash. Does your mom have a really silly pet name for him? Use it when absolutely necessary.

2. Ask your mother to give you two lunches. That way when he steals yours —

and he <u>will</u> steal yours even if he has his own — you'll still have something to eat.

③ Tell new kids and teachers that you have a very, very common last name, and that not everyone with the same last name in the school is related to you.

④ Try to explain to him that he's only acting like a bully in order to cover up for his own shortcomings and insecurities. And if that doesn't work, run until your sneakers are worn out.

⑤ Never let him smell your fear.

HOW TO TAKE POSSESSION OF THE REMOTE CONTROL WITHOUT LOSING A LIMB

The Civil War was fought over slavery. World War II was fought to preserve democracy from evil dictators. The Spanish-American War was fought because — well, I have no idea why the Spanish-American War was fought. But the point is that most of the wars fought in our house are fought over the remote control. Six people. A hundred channels. Only twenty-four hours in the day. You do the math. Here are some strategies to make sure you won't have to watch the ninety-nine channels you don't want to be watching.

1 Sew a pocket underneath the couch where you can keep the remote without anyone else ever finding it. Whenever you want to change a channel, gently

lean over, press your secret compart-
ment . . . and <u>voilà!</u> Comedy Central is all
yours.

2 Hide the remote control under your
shirt. Then, when your parents demand
to know where it is, tell them your
younger brother ate it. (In my family,
this is all too believable.)

3 Switch the stereo remote control for
the TV remote control and see if anyone
in your family can tell the difference.

4 Lick the remote control after you use
it, so nobody will want to touch it, let
alone change the channel after you.

5 When dealing with younger brothers or
dim older brothers, tell them they need
a secret password in order to use the
remote. No matter what they guess, tell
them they're wrong.

HOW TO CLEAN YOUR ROOM WITHOUT BREAKING A SWEAT

My mom has this thing about order: She loves giving orders, and she loves keeping everything in order. (My dad's the opposite; the only kind of order he likes is, "I'll have a burger and a super-size fries.") When our rooms are messy, it drives Mom even crazier than she already is. So it's best to clean when you can . . . preferably without having to do any work.

❶ Tell your little brother that he can use any of the dust clumps he finds to build a dustman (it's like a snowman, only filthy – perfect for little brothers).

❷ Finally, an indoor use for the snowblower that your father bought last winter and only used twice!

Wear the same clothes every day. It cuts down on clutter, which means less cleanup.

 Turn your bedroom into a science project. Tell your mother that cleaning it would destroy the ecosystem that you're trying to create.

 Tell your brother you've just invited the most beautiful girl in school over to study. See how fast his part of the mess disappears. I guarantee his drawers will be back in his drawers before you can say, "I see Paris, I see France. . . ."

HOW TO TRICK YOUR MOTHER INTO LETTING YOU STAY UP LATE

If God had wanted us to fall asleep at a certain time, he'd make us really tired at that time. Right?

1 Tell her that PBS is showing a really important documentary at midnight that you absolutely need to see for school.

2 Set all the clocks in the house back by two hours. If she notices, tell her it's two times the value of Daylight Savings Time.

3 Ask her about a time her parents let her stay up late . . . with any luck she'll get so nostalgic that she'll let you stay up, too.

4 Tell her you need time to ponder the wisdom she's shared with you over the course of the day.

Inform her that you're wired on too much caffeine and chocolate, and that if she doesn't let you release some energy, you might destroy your room in an insomniac fit.

Of course when I tried to use these excuses on my mom, the results were less than successful. In fact I think it went like this. . . .

(1) No teacher would ever assign a class to watch a TV show at home when he or she could show the same TV show in class over a whole week and not have to do a single lesson plan. (2) I wear a watch, Malcolm. (3) My parents never let me stay up late. Not once. They always said it had something to do with rising up early to harvest the crops. We didn't even have a backyard. (4) You want wisdom? I'll give you wisdom. GO TO SLEEP. (5) Whatever you do to your room, you'll have to clean up. Which is fine by me.

Maybe you'll have better luck . . . and if you do, let me know how!

HOW TO TRICK YOUR FATHER INTO LETTING YOU STAY UP LATE

Okay, so if it doesn't work with Mom, try with Dad. Odds are he'll like the company.

1 Tell him that there's a really important monster truck rally on cable that you absolutely need to see for school.

2 Set all the clocks in the house ahead by twelve hours. If he notices, tell him it's Daylight Swapping Time.

3 Ask him about a time his parents let him stay up late . . . and do your own thing as he spends the next five hours talking about the night his parents made him keep watch to make sure no thieving gnomes would get into the house while they were asleep.

4 Tell him you need more time to ponder the wisdom he's shared with you over the course of the day.

5 Inform him that you're wired on too much caffeine and chocolate, and that if he doesn't let you release some energy, you might start acting like a berserk killer robot.

<u>My dad buys all of these — especially the one about the gnomes.</u>

HOW TO COVER UP FOR BEING SMART

It isn't easy being a Krelboyne. Everybody assumes that just because you're smart, you'll act smart. But sometimes it doesn't work that way – believe me, I know. So on the days when I don't feel like being smart, here are some of the things I do.

1 Missspel thinks on porpoise. This dryvs teechers insain. Butt yu ken definitly hav sum fun with itt.

2 When people ask you what 89,562 x 98,641 equals, tell them it's 8,834,485,241, even though you know it's 8,834,485,242. That'll really throw them off.

3 Smuggle a blank piece of paper into a test and pretend you're using a cheat sheet, just to make your classmates feel better when the grades come out.

If your classmates want you to practice for the Math Olympics at recess, be sure to go out and play some football instead.

5 Everybody knows the line between being smart and being just plain weird is a very thin one. The next time someone calls you smart, yell, "Trams! Trams ton ma I" a few times. Odds are they'll leave you alone after that.

HOW TO ROLLER SKATE WITH GRACE AND EASE

I learned most of these skills from my father, who used to win all sorts of awards and break all sorts of hearts at the skating rink.

① Sing "That's the Way (uh-huh uh-huh) I Like It" (or some other great disco hit of the 1970s) to get yourself into the groove. Unless you're absolutely, positively alone, I advise you to sing it inside your head, not out loud.

② Be at one with the wheels.

③ If (2) doesn't work, just try to stay on your feet.

④ Never make eye contact with girls while you're skating. If you're already doing something stupid, this will only amplify it. And if you're not already doing something stupid, I guarantee that eye contact will make you suddenly do something of such gigantic stupidity that even you will be amazed by it.

5 Wear a helmet and knee pads. If you happen to be skating alongside my father, also wear a pillow duct-taped across your stomach, a mouthguard, protective eyewear, waterproof trousers, a back brace, and ankle bumpers. Have a pair of crutches and a wheelchair ready. Just in case.

HOW TO TRICK A BROTHER LIKE FRANCIS INTO ACHIEVING YOUR GOALS

Now, a brother like Francis is a King of trickery, so you have to be careful - if you use one of the old reliables, odds are that he's done it before and will be able to see right through it. So you have to be inventive if you want to make him do what you want him to do.

1. Let him believe he's your wise and noble guru in the ways of trickery and that any idea you have naturally springs from his wisdom.

2. If it will make him look good with <u>the ladies,</u> he's all yours.

3. Whether he's starting an alternative laundry at his school or playing a big-stakes game of pool, Francis loves a good get-rich scheme. He won't do any-

thing just for the money – but if you can convince him there's money <u>and</u> risk, he'll be on board in no time.

④ Convince him that whatever you're doing will strike back at the parents who sent him off to boarding school.

⑤ Blackmail. (You know every hiding place in his room.)

HOW TO TRICK A BROTHER LIKE REESE INTO ACHIEVING YOUR GOALS

You think it would make it easier to have a brother who's two beef patties short of a Big Mac. But sometimes clueless people are the hardest to get around, since their logic is just so . . . off. Here are some things you can do to make them go your way.

1. Pretend that the trick is really on someone else. For example, tell him that by cleaning up your room, he's really pulling a fast one on Mom.

2. Appeal to his sense of being all-powerful. "If you want people to think you're the toughest kid in the school, you'd better make sure nobody messes with your little brother." Soon you've got better protection than the President.

Baffle him completely. Be really, really unclear and he'll grasp the only clear thing around. Like this: "If the ergonomic properties of the gross national product were extrapolated into the prime integers drawn by Man Ray to the power of twelve, you should really take the garbage out."

4 Appeal to his desire to be smart. You're walking a fine line here — you need to refer to a famous smart person, but it has to be a famous smart person that your brother knows. (This usually eliminates everyone but Shakespeare and Einstein.) The thought process goes like this: If you say, "Einstein always gave his little brother the last french fries," a brother like Reese will think, Hey, if I give my little brother the last french fries, that means I'm just like freakin' Einstein. You'll get the french fries, and your brother will think he's a genius.

Blackmail. (Repeat after me: "I know what you did last summer....")

HOW TO TRICK A BROTHER LIKE DEWEY INTO ACHIEVING YOUR GOALS

Don't let the cute factor fool you – behind the huggable exterior lies a cunning mind bent on destruction and chaos. Proceed with caution. And remember – the way to his heart is through his digestive tract.

1 A peanut butter and hamburger sandwich

2 Vanilla ice cream with mustard sauce

3 An orange-juice-and-chocolate-syrup shake

4 Potato chip salad, with a creamy Velveeta dressing

5 A Happy Meal where you get to eat the fries and he gets to eat the toy

HOW TO GET OUT OF GOING IN FRONT OF THE WHOLE SCHOOL IN A COURT JESTER COSTUME

Most school plays are freak shows for the well-meaning. You wear clothes you'd never be caught dead in, say words no human being would ever say, and – to make matters worse – you have to do it in front of pretty much everyone you know. Some people call this acting, but I say it's just acting weird. Here's how to get out of it.

1 Trick your teacher into thinking you need daily visits to the school therapist. Once you get to his or her office, make up the craziest dreams you can. You'll soon have an unlimited hall pass.

2 Costumes for school plays are never made out of real fabric. The minute you try the costume on, scratch yourself frantically. Shiver and convulse, if necessary. Repeat until the teacher gives in and lets you wear jeans.

3 Pretend to have forgotten which part you're playing and say everyone else's lines instead of your own. Eventually, the teacher will become so frustrated that you'll be "promoted" to stage manager.

4 Along the same lines, no matter what play you're in, act as if it's <u>Grease</u>. A few carefully placed bars of "Greased Lightning" will send everything downhill fast.

5 Break a leg.

FIVE IRON-CLAD EXCUSES FOR GETTING AWAY WITH NOT DOING YOUR HOMEWORK

Especially when you have a family like mine, it isn't always easy to find the time to do homework. There are always more important things to do (like Play Station, or air hockey). So the next time you're a little short in the assignment department, be sure to use one of these fail-safe excuses. In my case, it helps that they're (mostly) true.

1. My father stole it so he could use it for his business presentation.

2. My little brother used it as TP.

3. I had to FedEx it to my older brother in boarding school so he could sell it to the highest bidder.

4. My mother accidentally baked it into last night's tuna casserole, and we digested it,

since my mother's tuna casserole usually tastes like a forty-page report on <u>Moby-Dick</u>.

5 The homework ate my dog.*

*- May you rest in peace, Charlie the Chihuahua - I had no idea you'd think my volcano was a safe place to sleep. . . .

FAKE A BOOK REPORT IN FIVE EASY STEPS

Now, don't get me wrong. Books can be cool. But it's very, very rare that the books you want to read are the ones the teacher assigns you.

1 Always read the last chapter. Even if you don't get to the rest of it, the last chapter will give you enough information to prove to the teacher that you read it. Of course, some authors like to sneak a major plot twist into the middle of the book, so you should probably read from the middle of the book until the end. Wait a minute! There are a few really sneaky authors who give you all kinds of important stuff in the first couple of chapters so you need to read those too. Okay, here's what you do: Read the beginning, the middle, and the end of the book. I guarantee you that you'll be able to prove to your teacher that you read the book. Understanding it is a whole other problem! (Hey, what are you complaining about? I never said all these ideas were foolproof.)

2 If the teacher asks you what you thought of the book, tell him or her that you found the book to be very "moving." They'll be so excited that the book actually meant something to you that they'll give you a better grade. (Bonus points if you can tell the teacher a specific detail from the last chapter that you found "moving," like: "It was really moving when Scrooge decided to back off on Tiny Tim's family" or "I was <u>extremely</u> moved when Odysseus got back home and found that Penelope had tricked the other guys into not hitting on her.") But again you have to be prepared to tell them how the book moved you and why. See, it's no good saying that the book was "moving" only to find out that it's really not because then not only does your teacher suggest that you go see the school psychologist, but the kids in your class will be <u>moving</u> to the other side of the room. Therefore, back to point one. Sorry, there doesn't seem to be a way out, does there?

③ Always talk about the three major conflicts: Man vs. Man (two people fight with each other), Man vs. Nature (there's a storm), or Man vs. Himself (the main guy thinks that maybe it wasn't a good idea to go after the whale). Teachers eat this stuff up.

④ Riff on the title. If the book's called <u>Great Expectations</u>, write about how great everyone's expectations were. If it's called <u>Death Be Not Proud,</u> mention that death isn't — you know — proud. And if it's called <u>A Tale of Two Cities</u> — well, let me give you a tip: It's probably about two cities.

5 If all else fails, I have a suggestion — it begins with the word "Cliff" and ends with the word "Notes."

HOW TO DEAL WITH AN EVIL GYM TEACHER

There are few things worse on this earth than a gym teacher who's out to get you. You know the type. They tend to sit in lawn chairs as they yell at you to do sit-ups (something they haven't been able to do themselves since the invention of the automobile). They use their whistles a lot. They never bother to learn your name. Well, you can't let them get away with their evil. Here's how to cope.

1 Fake elaborate medical excuses. If you forge a note saying you only have two weeks to live, odds are they'll let you sit out the whole year.

2 Change the rules. You need the cooperation of your classmates on this one, but if a gym teacher is truly evil, you shouldn't have much problem getting them to sign on. The idea is simple –

alter the game. For example, when you're playing baseball, make sure everyone runs to third base first. When the teacher questions this, innocently say, "But that's how the game is played" and have all your teammates back you up. The gym teacher's head will explode.

3 Invent your own sports to play, like "The fifty-minute lie-down" or "carrycomicball," which (as everyone knows) involves carrying a ball down to the nearest convenience store and buying a comic book to read for the rest of the class.

4 Get out of gym by repeatedly taking the period to see your guidance counselor. If your evil gym teacher questions this, tell him you're just trying to choose a college really, really early.

5 If all else fails, a little glue on the whistle never hurts. . . .

HOW TO GET SPONSORS FOR A CHARITY EVENT

Scamming money for a charity is a no-lose situation: The money goes to a good place, and you look really good giving it. But some people are very reluctant to let go of their cash, even if it helps build a community center, feed starving children, or send the school's tuba squad on a trip to Bosnia. Here's how to break through their greed and get to the good.

1 If you happen to have a friend in a wheelchair (like I do), wheel him door to door to ask for help. When people see a wheelchair, they tend to feel guilty, like they were the ones who put your friend there in the first place. Because of this guilt, they pay up.

2 Start crying if they try to turn you away. It might be a little embarrassing, but they'll do just about anything to get you off their doorstep.

3 Let them know your older brother is the neighborhood bully. They might consider a donation to be like protection money.

4 The next time their pet is alone in the yard, scoop it up in your arms, ring the front doorbell, and tell the residents that their pet was lost a long way from home and that you found it and brought it back. At first, tell them you don't need any monetary reward. But if they persist (and odds are they will), take the money and run.

5 Sing them songs from Cats. Everyone loves Cats.

HOW TO GET AWAY WITH WRITING YOUR FAMOUS AMERICAN IN HISTORY REPORT ON A RACE CAR DRIVER

John Adams. Harriet Tubman. Jeff Gordon. Who would you rather write about? If your teacher asks why you've gone the race car route, point out these things:

1 Race car drivers make more money than presidents.

2 Race car drivers are on the front of cereal boxes – unlike, say, Eleanor Roosevelt.

3 Race car drivers have big fan clubs. I don't think Lincoln had a fan club.

4 Sure, what Lewis and Clark did was impressive. But it would have been much more impressive if they'd done it at 170 mph.

5 Like the Founding Fathers, race car drivers are all about life, liberty, and the pursuit of happiness. The only difference is that they wear cool outfits covered with big-name product endorsements.

HOW TO BUILD AN EFFECTIVE ALIBI (FOR ANYTHING)

There are few things in life that are worse than getting caught. An effective alibi is something you need to get out of such scrapes. Even if there was no one around to say you didn't do it, there are ways to put yourself in the clear. Here's how to build an effective alibi.

1 Swap alibis with someone else who needs one. (Sample: "Dad, if you tell Mom that I was in here all afternoon and couldn't have possibly been the one who accidentally defrosted the refrigerator and ruined all the stuff in it, I'll tell Mom that you were with me all morning and couldn't have possibly been the one who left the iron on in the closet and burned half her clothes.")

Memorize your <u>TV Guide</u>. If your brother asks, "Hey, who messed up my baseball cards?" be prepared to summarize all the television programs you were watching while his room was left unattended.

❸ Switch the clocks. In my house this is easy, since none of the clocks match up. Thus, if you happen to knock over a vase at five o'clock in the living room, you can be safe in your room at five o'clock, ten minutes later.

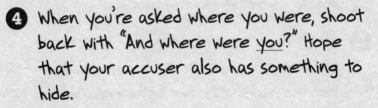

❹ When you're asked where you were, shoot back with "And where were <u>you</u>?" Hope that your accuser also has something to hide.

❺ Hire a good lawyer.

HOW TO GET OUT OF GOING TO THE PRINCIPAL'S OFFICE

The good news is: You're out of class. The bad news is: You're on the road to detention. Here's how to stay off that road . . . and keep out of class.

1. Befriend the principal's secretary. They hold the real power, and if you show them that you know it, they're more willing to use it in your favor.

2. Try to get in trouble in the last three minutes of class; that way, you can amble the halls until the bell rings. Then, technically, you're free to go to your next class. (It's in the United Nations Rules of International Detention. I swear.)

Keep your test scores high. If you're keeping up the school's average, the principal isn't going to do a thing to you.

 Compliment the principal's clothes. A principal gets so few compliments throughout the day, that one little kind word makes all the difference.

 When the principal says to me, "I'm going to call your parents," I always ask him, "Do you really want to have to deal with my mom?" He usually puts the phone down pretty quick after that.

HOW TO EAT WELL IN THE SCHOOL CAFETERIA

Think it's not possible? Think you're stuck eating another portion of ratatouille (which is French for "yesterday's garbage served warm")? Well, think again. This is how to get away with eating well in the cafeteria.

 Don't be a dodo – stick with the Ho-Hos. Even the cafeteria can't ruin prepackaged snack cakes.

 Barter. Just as the ancient tribes swapped antelope skins for butter, find people who will share some of their Doritos for some of your pretzel sticks. This will give you more variety for your buck.

 As alluded to above, remember the five major cafeteria food groups: Snack Cakes, Bag Chips, Beverage of Choice (chocolate milk or soda, where available),

Dubious Meatstuff (with or without Alfredo Sauce), and Pizza. Pizza, of course, dominates all other food groups — the times when it's available (roughly once in a blue moon), eat up.

4 Fried is good. It doesn't matter if it's fish, cheese, chicken, orange rinds, or a shoe — when the cafeteria fries something, it always tastes the same. So just choose your favorite fried entree and pretend that whatever you're eating is it. Trust me — your taste buds'll never know the difference.

5 Make nice to the cafeteria ladies. Most of them are moms, you know. Appeal to that maternal side and suddenly you'll have them saving the last slices of pizza for you.

HOW TO ~~DEAL~~ WITH ~~A~~ NERVOUS TEACHER

Teachers have a lot to deal with - you know, kids like you and me. Some teachers handle it a little better than others. You have the military-style dictators who cover over their insecurities with a lot of shout-ing and orders. You have the touchy-feely teachers who can't figure out whether they want to be your teacher or your pal. And then you have the teachers who are always on the verge of cracking. It's not a pretty sight, but it can have its advantages if you work it right.

1. Know where she keeps her cell phone and know which speed-dial number is her therapist's (it's usually #1).

2. Monitor her clothing. If it's too bright or too black, you're in for a rough day.

3 Humor her. If she wants the class to act out the complete works of Shakespeare while standing on desks, why not?

4 Be aware that she is probably very concerned about her job security. If you're extra well behaved when the principal sits in on your class, you'll be able to ask her for your college recommendations years ahead of time.

5 Be nice. Learning to deal with crazy, neurotic, and/or wacky people is a much much more important life skill than finding the hypotenuse of an acute triangle.

HOW TO USE THE FACT THAT YOUR FRIENDS ARE GEEKS TO YOUR ADVANTAGE

Yes, a lot of my friends are, um, socially challenged. They'd make a lousy baseball team and an even-worse episode of <u>The Real World</u>. But they are good for other things. Having geeks as friends definitely has its upside.

1 Have them record TV shows for you. They're always home.

2 Their homework is always done. Neatly. And they're always early for school. So take that ten minutes of quality time to bum some answers off of them, or at least make sure that your answers are right.

3 Their parents are usually so thrilled that they have friends that they're willing to take you places and spend money on you that your own parents would never dream of doing. I have to beg and plead to get my parents to rent a movie I want to see. But when I go over to some Krelboyne's house, his parents are more than willing to make it a Blockbuster night — popcorn, La-Z Boy recliners . . . the works. (On the downside, Krelboyne parents can be a little overprotective — but we find ways to get around that.)

4 They always have a calculator handy. This makes figuring out things like tips really easy.

5 They are able and willing to create the most insane projects (remote control lamps, ultra-aerodynamic water balloons), all in the name of science.

HOW TO BABY-SIT YOUR BROTHER WITHOUT MAJOR INCIDENT — IF HE'S ANYTHING LIKE DEWEY

I know I'm not the greatest expert at this. Things tend to disappear, blow up, or get the attention of angry neighbors whenever I baby-sit. But there are some things I've learned that I think can help pull off a baby-sitting job without ending up in a sirened vehicle.

1 Keep an eye on your little brother or sister at all times. I mean it. Don't turn your back. Try not to blink. If you have to go to the kitchen for a snack, take him with you. If you have to go to the bathroom, stick him in the bathtub while you do. Otherwise, he'll vanish faster than you can say, "My parents are going to kill me!"

2 The television is a baby-sitter's best friend. You are being paid to let him have the remote control. Go with it. There's no way you can keep him as occupied as your cable-ready friend can.

3 Stay away from balloons. If you let your brother near one, he will chase it to the ends of the earth — or, at the very least, to a bad part of town.

4 Try to avoid changing diapers. Especially if your brother's seven.

5 If your brother offers you something to eat, DO NOT TAKE IT. You have no idea where it's been.

HOW TO KEEP IN TOUCH WITH YOUR OLDER BROTHER AFTER HE'S BEEN SENT AWAY TO BOARDING SCHOOL

I love my brother Francis. The house hasn't been the same since he was shipped away. So what if he caused a few hundred thousand dollars in damage while he was here? It wasn't <u>always</u> his fault. (He's so misunderstood.) Anyway, places like his school aren't exactly phone-call friendly. So sometimes you have to take matters into your own hands. . . .

1 If you're sending a care package, always use a church as the return address.

2 Arrange times for him to call collect when your parents aren't home. By the time the bill comes, they probably won't remember they weren't home, and will assume they were the ones who talked to him.

3 Carrier pigeons are only effective if your brother's school doesn't have a shooting range.

4 Develop a phone code for when your parents are around. Press 3 before any statement you're making because your mom is hovering behind you (e.g., "Things are great here" and "You just missed the best dinner"). Press 6 if you are passing on family gossip he's not supposed to know, and press 9 if you are about to be shooed off the phone but still have things to tell him. Finally, press 2 if you have been suspended from school, or any other thing you can't say out loud for fear of being overheard.

5 Send postcards from home that say "Wish You Were Here" - he'll get the point.

HOW TO REACT WHEN YOUR FATHER FINDS YOU'VE BEEN BORROWING SMALL AMOUNTS FROM HIS WALLET

1 Tell him you heard a strange voice in your head – a cross between Elmer Fudd and Hannibal Lecter – instructing you to take the money. Now that the voice is gone, you promise you won't do it again.

2 Convince him it's not really his wallet, it's only the wallet that the government wants him to believe is his.

3 Tell him he's paying you back for the embarrassment he caused the time he showed up for your fifth-grade beach trip wearing a thong and flip-flops.

4 Let him know that if he doesn't let you keep the money, you'll tell your mother he said she was looking "a little on the

chunky side lately." If he has any sense
of self-preservation, he'll soon be
handing you the whole wallet.

 Inform him gently that the money is actually yours; you've just been keeping it
in his wallet temporarily.

HOW TO REACT WHEN YOUR MOTHER FINDS YOU'VE BEEN BORROWING SMALL AMOUNTS FROM HER WALLET

1 Pray hard.

2 Run hard.

3 Repent quick.

4 Prepare a list of make-it-up-to-you chores.

5 Be prepared to pay interest.

HOW TO SURVIVE LONG FAMILY CAR RIDES

Can you imagine being trapped in a tiny room with your whole family, with no way to leave to get food or go to the bathroom? Well, that's a family car ride for you. No escape. No patience. Here's how to make it through.

1 Wear headphones. (Duh.)

2 If your parents forbid you to wear headphones, shout out Eminem's greatest hits really, really loud. They'll let you wear headphones soon enough.

3 Count blue cars. It'll give you something to do. Or it will put you to sleep. Both are good.

4 If there are no blue cars around, count the number of times your mother says <u>where</u> ("Where are you going?" "Where are we?" "Where do you get off trying to change the radio station while Barry Manilow is playing?") and the number of times your father says <u>what</u> ("What do you want me to do?" "What did that sign say?" "What is wrong with steering with my feet?")

5 If you multiply the number of times your mother says <u>where</u> and your father says <u>what</u> by the miles you've traveled and the minutes it has taken, you will have your Car Ride Misery Index. If your CRMI is over 500, it's time to lobby for a portable DVD player instead of the headphones.

HOW TO PRETEND YOU'RE SICK AND HAVE YOUR MOM FALL FOR IT

Until "I really don't feel like it" is an acceptable excuse for missing school, you're going to have to rely on the tried-and-true method of pretending you're sick.

1 Put the thermometer on the radiator or lightbulb – remembering to take it off before the temperature reaches 106°. One time I forgot and got rushed to the hospital with a 125° temperature, which I think would make me legally dead. Oops.

2 Stick to your story. Usually, you have two options: cold or flu. If you opt for cold, don't complain of a stomachache. If you opt for flu, don't tell her you have a stuffy nose. Know your symptoms.

③ Piggyback on other's sickness. If your brothers or parents are sick, imitate their symptoms and get to stay home, too. The downside is you're stuck in a house with sick people for the whole day.

④ Invent your own illness. Some of my favorites:

Moravian Flu: Lots of dry coughs and moans

Elephant Pox: If you knock your elbow, turn the resulting bump into a reason to stay home

Early Morning Sleep Disorder: i.e., inability to wake up on time

Pre-Examatic Test Syndrome: The test's today and you forgot to study last night

Sports Day-itis: This one is easy – just limp. It's really useful on the days when you're being forced to wear gym shorts in front of the whole school and do things like the long jump or running sprints

 Make yourself sick worrying whether or not your mother is going to believe you're sick.

<u>Once again, none of this actually works on my mom, but . . .</u>

HOW TO PRETEND YOU'RE SICK AND HAVE YOUR FATHER FALL FOR IT

Moms are stuck on the whole medical side of being sick. With Dads (well, at least my dad), you can rely on the bigger picture. That is, you don't actually have to have a temperature of 103° in order to convince him that you can't go to school. Here are five quick steps to staying home. My dad falls for them mostly because he's been there himself.

1. Whenever your dad talks to you, call him "mommy." No matter how many times he corrects you, still call him "mommy."

2. Very slowly, use your forefinger to tap yourself on the nose. Repeat for as long as it takes. If your father asks you why you're tapping your nose, tell him you don't know what he's talking about.

3 Keep your head in a pillow to make it hot and clammy. Then, when your father asks you what's wrong, simply say, "I am Spartacus."

4 If he tells you to go to school, tell him that today in science class, you're dissecting aliens, and that you want to stay home on principle – and out of the fear that if you dissect an alien, the next time an alien abducts you, he'll dissect you, too.

5 If all else fails, ask him if he wants to go to a monster truck rally. Odds are he'll call in sick himself and keep you out of school. (This only works if your mother is already out of the house.)

HOW TO EFFECTIVELY PASS THE BUCK

Here are some pointers for when you're snagged red-handed and an alibi won't work.

① Cite precedent. This is a legal term for saying, "The last time I did this, you let me off. So it would be unfair of you to snag me now." For example, the next time your father catches you making a prank call, remind him that the last time you made a prank call (to his boss), he was pleased.

② Create a diversion. Say your mother catches you snarfing down some ice cream a few minutes before dinner. Right when she's about to holler, say, "Is that the sound of someone choking?" (or some such thing).*

③ Figure out who's not around. Blame him. ("Someone took a few dollars from the laundry money? I hate to say this, but I did see Grandpa snooping around there. He hasn't been here for the past few months? Well, are you sure you've checked it since then?")

4 Pets are perfect creatures to pass the buck to. If, for example, you were to crash your mom's favorite vase to the floor, be sure to yell, "Bad Rover! Look what you've done!" at the top of your lungs. Note: This only works if you have a pet. I once tried to blame my neighbor's pet, but my mom didn't buy it.

5 Take full responsibility. If you do this in my house, it will be assumed that you're covering up for someone else. Thus, you'll get away with it.

* Note: This doesn't work with my mom, but maybe you're lucky and it will work for you.

HOW TO COME UP WITH A KILLER HISTORY PROJECT

I'm sure you've had that moment when you think to yourself, If I have to do another diorama of Thomas Edison inventing the lightbulb, I'll SCREAM!!! (Unless you can use the same diorama over and over again — then it's cool.) The next time your history teacher asks for a report, try one of these exciting topics.

1. The Donner Party (they ate one another, you know)

2. The Titanic (if you rent the movie and take out the love stuff, that's research)

3. Alexander the Great (because he was young and he got his way)

4. World War II (talk to your grandfather for an hour, write it down, call it an "oral history," get an A+)

5 King Arthur (major swordplay is great for class presentations)

HOW TO TALK TO A GIRL WITHOUT MAKING A TOTAL FOOL OF YOURSELF

Most of these things I learned from my brother Francis. He's an expert on the subject. I still find girls frustrating, cool, unpredictable, exasperating, great, terrifying, cute — in other words, both a dream and a nightmare. Whenever I talk to a girl, I feel that there's a big, fat sign on my head that says, LOSER ALERT. Here's how to get around it.

1 Rehearse your words. But don't rehearse them out loud, because then she'll hear them.

2 If you're complimenting her on a piece of clothing that's above her waist and you don't know what it is (shirt, blouse, sweater, etc.), use the word "top." As in, "That's a great top, Suzie."

3 If you're complimenting her on a piece of clothing that's below her waist, don't call it a "bottom." Trust me.

4 This isn't second grade anymore. Making fun of a girl isn't the way to her heart.

5 Don't invite the girl over to your house until you've prepared her to meet your family. If you don't, she might see your dad in his underwear, trip on garbage, and end up in tears. Not a good way to start.

HOW TO RECOVER AFTER YOU'VE TALKED TO A GIRL AND MADE A TOTAL FOOL OF YOURSELF

I learned most of these things from my brother Francis, too. Unfortunately, he's also an expert on <u>this</u> subject. So here's what to do when you face the crash and burn instead of a smooooooth landing.

1 Don't try to cover things up. Blaming the guy next to you isn't going to make her like you more.

2 Don't try to explain things unless you know what the explanation is. (I call this the "ummm . . . uh . . . well . . . you know" phenomenon.)

3 If at first you don't succeed, <u>don't</u> run away without saying another word. (I am <u>so</u> guilty of this crime. Or, even worse, I wait so long to reply that the girl's gone before I can say another word.)

4 Taking it all back never works, either.

5 Be sweet. Because you're a guy, odds are that girls are expecting the worst from you (and hoping for the best). The best way to disarm them is to actually act nice. This goes a long way.

HOW TO KEEP YOUR MOTHER HAPPY

You'd be amazed how far these things can get you.

1 Remember her birthday. (Bonus points if you remember to buy her a present. Sticks of bubble gum or cards written on a piece of paper torn from your bio notebook DON'T COUNT.)

2 Remind your dad about her birthday. (Anniversaries work well here, too.)

3 When you're visiting her at work, don't pull apart any of the displays, don't make gaseous noises while she's on the phone, and don't call her boss "Loser-boy" unless that happens to be his proper name.

4 Say "thank you" as much as you can. Unless she's just punished you. Then she'll

think you're being sarcastic and will pun-
ish you some more.

⑤ Every once in a while, do something she
asks you to the first time she asks. Just
for shock value.

HOW TO KEEP YOUR FATHER HAPPY

Yes, you'll risk embarrassment ... sometimes <u>extreme</u> embarrassment. But if your dad is anything like my dad, these simple things can make all the difference in the world.

① Learn to speak the arcane sports lexicon of his choice. For example, if your father happens to be obsessed with curling (okay, maybe your dad isn't like my dad in this respect), nod enthusiastically when he sits you down in front of the Ottawa Curling Semi-Finals and says, "Did you see the way he reached the twelve-foot ring in front of the tee-line by using such a gorgeous front house weight?"

② When he puts "I Got You Babe" on his karaoke machine, be Cher to his

Sonny – because you love him, and because it means so much to him.

③ Don't charge too much to be his alibi when he does something that Mom will kill him for. (Like, say, throwing his red fishing shirt in the laundry with her favorite white shirt.)

④ Pretend you've never heard the story about the time he and his best friend, Lou, went ice-fishing on a lake, only it was July so they nearly drowned. Even if he's telling you for the five-hundred-thirty-sixth time.

⑤ Take him to Career Day at school even if he doesn't have a job. Because, let's face it, being your dad is probably job enough.

HOW TO KEEP AN OLDER BROTHER LIKE FRANCIS HAPPY

So far away . . . and yet so close to the heart of our family. How can you make a long-distance brother relationship work? Try these simple steps.

1 Every time your parents enter the room, break down in tears. When they ask you what's wrong, moan out, "It's just that (sniff, sniff) I miss Francis (choke, choke) SO MUCH! (noseblow, noseblow). Why oh why (dramatic guilt-inducing glance) did you have to send him away?!?"

2 If you see his ex-girlfriend walking down the street with her new boyfriend, be sure to go up to her and say, "Hey, Francis got your letter last week, and can't wait to see you when he gets home!" (If the new boyfriend is a football star, run away immediately after saying this.)

3 If he sneaks home in order to see this ex-girlfriend, shelter him even though he's being ridiculous.

4 Help build his legend. When kids spread rumors that he ran away from home and is now a rodeo rider on the western plains, deny nothing. Act like everything mysterious is the truth.

5 Let him know that you really do miss him, and that you really do wish your parents would let him come home soon. (Bonus points if you can get this across in a totally nongreeting-card way.)

HOW TO KEEP AN OLDER BROTHER LIKE REESE OUT OF YOUR FACE

It's not as simple as feeding him raw meat and letting him think he's a six-foot-two Terminator when the truth is that he's really the size of a broom. No, there are deeper psychological needs that you have to deal with in order to make a brother like Reese happy. If you really want to enter a mind where the biggest question is "Should I get fries with that?", here are the keys:

1 When he has a crush on a girl, gently point out that relentlessly throwing water balloons at her probably isn't the way to her heart. Copy a Shakespeare sonnet for him to give to her. (Bonus: He'll think you wrote it.)

2 Let him think the older brother is always right, even though you know it's the <u>smarter</u> brother who's always right. (Well, most of the time.)

3 When he's having a really bad day, let him beat you at Mortal Kombat. Once.

4 Let him do all the destructive chores.

5 Don't make a deal about it, but let him know you appreciate the fact that he keeps the other big kids from picking on you.

HOW TO KEEP A LITTLE BROTHER LIKE DEWEY HAPPY

My brother Dewey doesn't ask for much . . . but when he <u>does</u> ask for something, you know about it. Believe me. Hurricanes and tornadoes are nothing compared to his tantrums. So in order to avoid a natural disaster, I'd encourage you to take the following steps.

1 Hold his hand while crossing the street.

2 If his new goal in life is getting a Sleepy Bedtime Herbie doll (now with super sleepy fuzzy fur), help him slowly wear down your parents' resistance.

3 Let him use one of your shoe boxes for his dried booger collection.

4 Don't freak out when you realize he's given each of his dried boogers a name.

Make sure to play games with him. Sometimes it's easy for the youngest kid to be forgotten.

HOW TO KEEP YOUR SISTER HAPPY

How should I know? Sorry, but you're on your own here.

HOW TO DRESS IN HAND-ME-DOWNS WITHOUT LOSING YOUR SELF-ESTEEM

My parents firmly believe in recycling . . . when it comes to clothes. From Francis to Reese to me, right down to Dewey, they will pass down clothes until there's only a single thread left. Now if you've never been in this kind of situation, you might think that it would lead to some cool, retro outfits. Wrong! Instead you get sleeves where noses have been blown, waistlines that are all line and no waist, and mysterious, green, furry lumps in the pockets (they once were sandwiches, back when your oldest brother was in third grade). Here's how to deal:

1 Think ahead. If your older brother has a spectacularly hideous shirt that you'd never want to be caught dead in (or alive, for that matter), go on the offensive and try to ruin it beyond repair while it's still in his possession. That way he gets blamed, and you won't have to wear it.

2 Swap hand-me-downs with your friends who are also little brothers. Yeah, the clothes you get will still have broken zippers, missing buttons, and collars that were born to choke, but at least you won't be wearing the same thing in your class picture that your whole family wore when they were your age.

3 Better yet, swap clothes with your friends who are older brothers or only children. Granted, there's not much in it for them. Except they're probably pretty tired of being seen with you in your out-of-date duds . . . and are willing to sacrifice a few of their shirts so they don't have to smell the decade-old sweat stains.

4 Pray you will grow much, much bigger than your brothers. If the clothes don't fit, then your parents have to quit.

5 At the very least, refuse to wear hand-me-downs that have your older sib's name on them. Same goes true for T-shirts with dated phrases on it – just because my brother Francis went to an Ace of Base concert ten years ago doesn't mean I have to wear the shirt from it now. Right?

My mom says Ace of Base are the Abba of my time. Who's ABBA?
Dad offered to take the shirt off my hands and wear it to Teacher Night at school, or maybe to the class picnic. . . . It was an offer no sane person would accept!

WHAT TO DO AFTER YOU HIT A BASEBALL THROUGH YOUR NEIGHBOR'S WINDOW

I think it would be safe to say that my neighbors aren't about to start a Malcolm fan club anytime soon. But what can I do? Our backyard isn't the biggest in the world, so sometimes the neighbor's window ends up being center field. Of course, the first thing you should do is run or blame the nearest relative. But if that doesn't work, try out these five catchphrases, guaranteed to save your skin.

1. "You should save that ball, because when I become famous it will be worth a lot on eBay."

2. "Did you see how that baseball just fell from the sky?!? There must be a _really_ amazing player in the next town over."

3 "Just think – if you board up that window, you'll never have to look at our house again!"

4 "If I let you throw a baseball through our window, will you consider us even?"

5 "Are you sure that's a baseball and not a spherical probe from another planet? I'd be careful how you touch it. You never know what might come out."

HOW TO SNEAK INTO AN ARCADE WITHOUT GETTING CAUGHT

You wouldn't think arcades would try to keep kids out — I mean, who do they think their customers are, senior citizens? But sometimes there's a guy at the door who instantly becomes the one roadblock between you and an hour or two of video game bliss. (Especially if you're supposed to be at school at the time.) Here's how to get past.

1 Bribe the bouncer with a few tokens.

2 Tell him you're training for the video Olympics, and your coach will be on his case if he doesn't let you in to practice.

3 Inform him that your math teacher has sent you on an assignment to measure the rate of quarter expenditure against the rate of high scores. (It helps if you have the ability to do these equations in your head and baffle the bouncer into submission.)

4 Create a diversion (for example, have a friend point around the corner and scream, "Isn't that a swimsuit model?!?") and run inside while the bouncer's distracted.

5 There's always the back door.

HOW TO CONTROL
YOUR MOM'S MIND

I haven't cracked this one yet. Perhaps you could help?

_____

_____

_____

_____

_____

_____

_____

_____

_____

_____

HOW TO MAKE YOUR SCHOOL A BETTER PLACE

I'm not talking about improved recycling here (not that there's anything wrong with recycling). I'm talking about the things that really matter—like getting rid of homework and bringing back nap time. How can we pull that off?

_____

_____

_____

_____

_____

_____

_____

_____

HOW TO THROW A SUCCESSFUL BIRTHDAY PARTY WITHOUT HAVING ANY MEMBER OF YOUR FAMILY RUIN IT

I cant' even make it past blowing out the candles before something happens. One year, my dad set his shirt on fire. Another year, Dewey ate the candles while they were still lit. The next year, Reese decided to light them with a flamethrower (and it was an ice-cream cake). How 'bout you give me some tips for pulling a birthday party off without major embarrassment or injury?

_____

_____

_____

_____

HOW TO CONVIENCE YOUR PARENTS TO GET A PET

We're like the roach motel of families - pets come in, but they don't come out. It's not intentional, I swear! I think it would be cool to have a dog. If you were me, how would you convince my parents to get one?

_____

_____

_____

_____

_____

_____

_____

_____

If you enjoyed this book, then don't miss these other great *Malcolm in the Middle* books:

#1: LIFE IS UNFAIR

Meet Malcolm. People used to think he was weird. But ever since his school put him in a special class for brainiacs—they KNOW he is.

Good thing his family is so normal. Wait—that must be someone ELSE's family.

#2: THE WATER PARK

Malcolm's family is taking a trip to a water park—it's one of the few public places that they're still allowed inside. Of course, when Malcolm and Reese start a war of practical jokes and revenge, that's going to change.

#3: THE BAD LUCK CHARM

Malcolm and Reese buy a stuffed monkey at a garage sale. They're planning to use it to scare Dewey, but the monkey's got other ideas. See, this monkey is bad luck—seriously—and when bad things start happening, Malcolm's brains and Reese's brawn aren't going to help them.

#4: THE EXCHANGE STUDENT

Malcolm's family is hosting an exchange student for a week. Her name is Camelia. She's Malcolm's age and just as smart. In addition, she's as tough as Reese, as cute as Dewey—she's even got Mom and Dad won over. She must be stopped!

#5: MALCOLM FOR PRESIDENT

Malcolm's been tricked into running for class president. He doesn't want the job but with a campaign manager like Reese he just might win. Can Malcolm get out of it before he becomes the first Krelboyne elected to office? Or will he catch election fever and decide to do whatever it takes to win?

#6: THE HOSTAGE CRISIS

Some dumb duo thought they were taking Malcolm's family hostage. Yeah, right. Now the criminals are trapped in the house with Reese, Dewey, and Malcolm, while the police are trapped outside with Lois and Hal. It's hard to know who to feel sorrier for.

#7: THE KRELBOYNE PARROT

It's Malcolm's turn to look after the Krelboyne class pet—an obnoxious parrot named Hitchcock. But then Hitchcock meets the ultimate vacuum cleaner and suddenly it's bye-bye birdie. What's a kid to do?

Can Malcolm face his class? Can he convince Reese to keep his mouth shut? And worst of all, can he keep it a secret from his mom?

Do you know Malcolm's shoe size? IQ? His best friend's name?

If you do, you really need to get out more. If you don't, this game has all the answers. Even if you miss a question you get to do totally cool challenges—like thumb wrestling and burping. (But don't tell mom or it's back into the closet for this game!)

So, check it out. It's great for two or more Malcolm fans, ages 8 and up.

Available nationally at Toys "R" Us and Target Stores.

www.fox.com/malcolminthemiddle

MALLICO2